W9-AZM-258

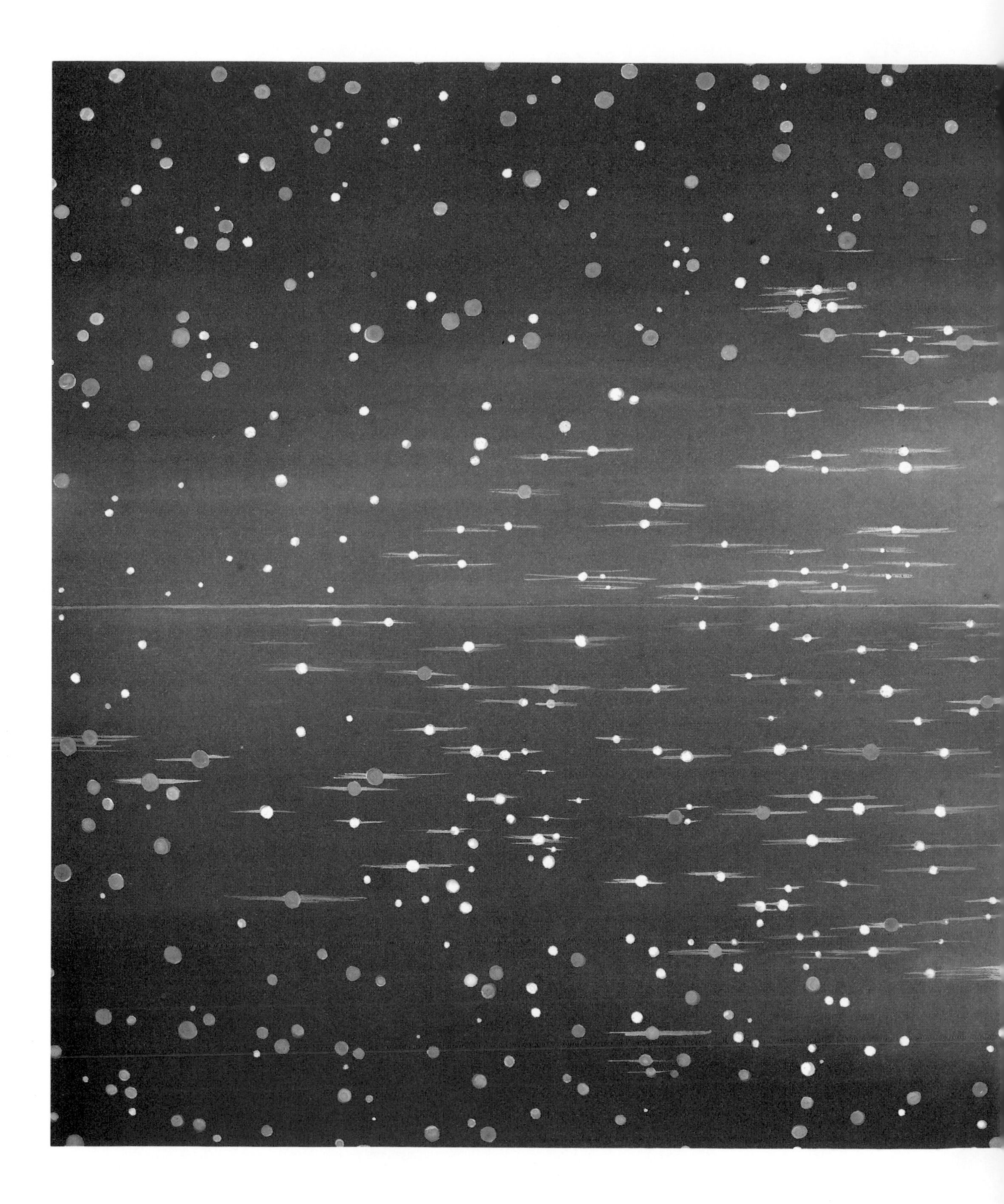

Ann Jonas

Reflections

Greenwillow Books, New York

This is for Don

Library of Congress Cataloging-in-Publication Data
Jonas, Ann. Reflections.
Summary: Chronicles a child's busy day by the sea, in a forest, at a carnival, and then to dinner and a concert. The illustrations change when the book is turned upside down.
1. Toy and movable books—Specimens. [1. toy and movable books] I. Title.
PZ7.J664Re 1987 [E] 86-33545 ISBN 0-688-06140-0 ISBN 0-688-06141-9 (lib. bdg.)

Manufactured in China by South China Printing Co. Ltd.
First Edition 09 10 11 12 13 SCP 20 19 18 17 16 15 14 13
Watercolor paintings were reproduced in full color. The typeface is Helvetica Regular.

After that it's time for bed.

The best place I know is here by the sea.

Later we all go to the park for the band concert.

There's so much to do. I get up at dawn.

From there we can watch the sun set.

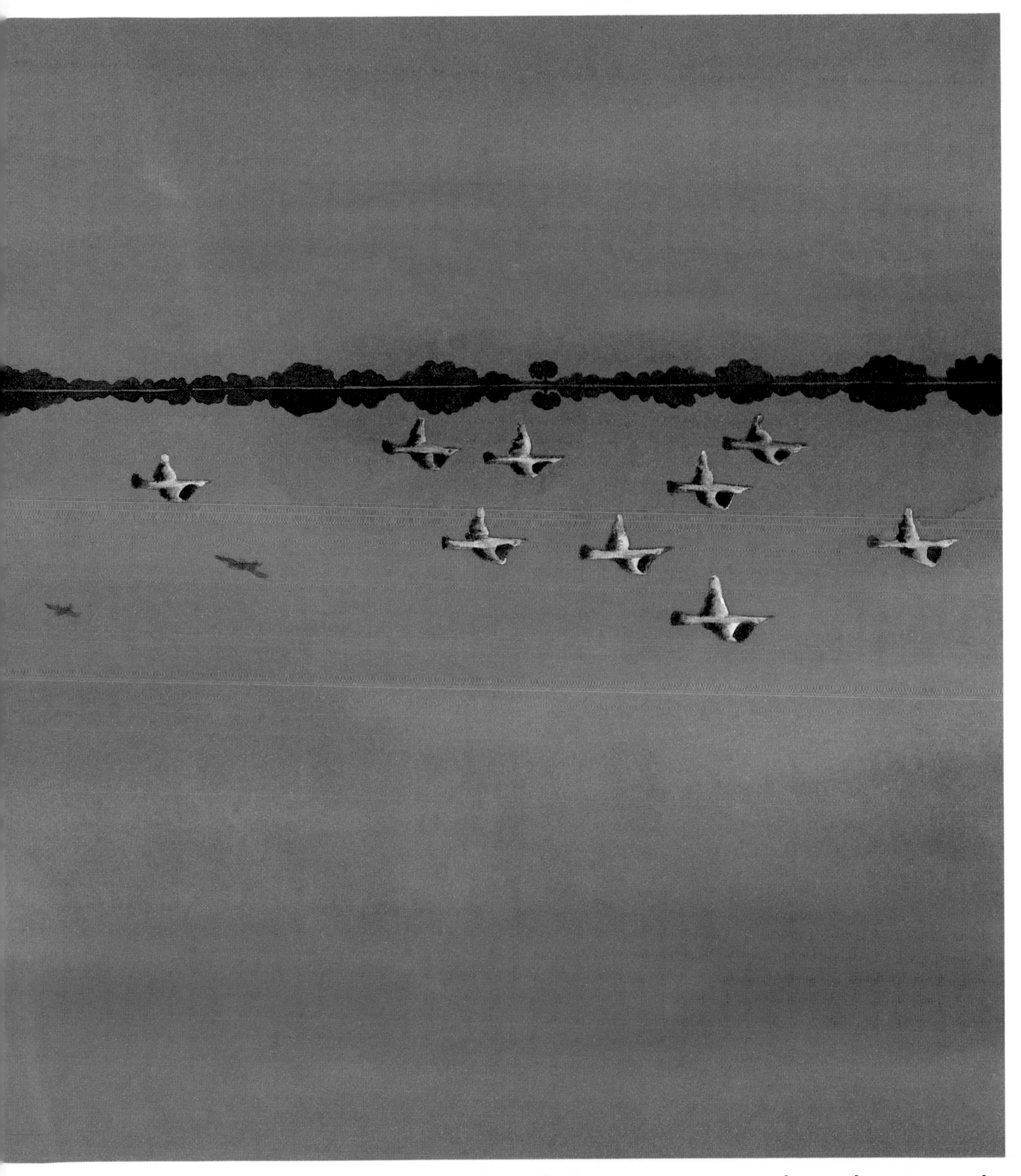

The fishermen are already at work.

easisea

Then we have dinner at the restaurant.

But I'm always in time to see the first ferry.

When it's windy enough, my family flies kites.

Sometimes a storm comes up on the bay.

I feed the ducks. They're always waiting.

It rains for a while. Then the sun comes out again.

The campground is empty. Everyone's at the beach.

I go to the boatyard, but no one's around.

They're all at the beach. It's too crowded for me.

Then I go back to the beach, but it's still too crowded.

The carnival is here at last. I take a ride.

So I take a walk up past the mill.

or even a fish if I'm really quick.

There's an orchard there, and the peaches are ripe.

Sometimes I catch a frog in the pond,

And in the birch grove there may be a deer.

It's a little scary deep in the woods, so I turn around–

and find my way back.

...TER A LIGHTNING CHANGE HAS TRANSFORMED ...E SCARLET SPEEDSTER BEFORE THE ...TARTLED EYES OF HIS GREEN-GARBED FRIEND...
BARRY ALLEN--THE "LAZY" BOY FRIEND OF IRIS WEST!
THE SAME! BUT NOW I THINK YOU'D BETTER GET OUT OF YOUR UNIFORM TOO, GL! WE'VE GOT SOME TALL EXPLAINING TO DO...
SHORTLY...
...AND SOMEHOW WE WANDERED OFF... AND GOT LOST...
THAT'S OUR STORY AND WE'RE STICKIN... TO IT!

LOST, eh? WELL, LET ME TELL YOU, HAL JORDAN, I'M NOT LETTING YOU OUT OF MY SIGHT FOR THE REST OF THIS WEEK END!
THAT SUITS ME FINE, CAROL!
YOU GOT LOST, eh? WELL, IF THAT DOESN'T SOUND JUST LIKE YOU, BARRY ALLEN!

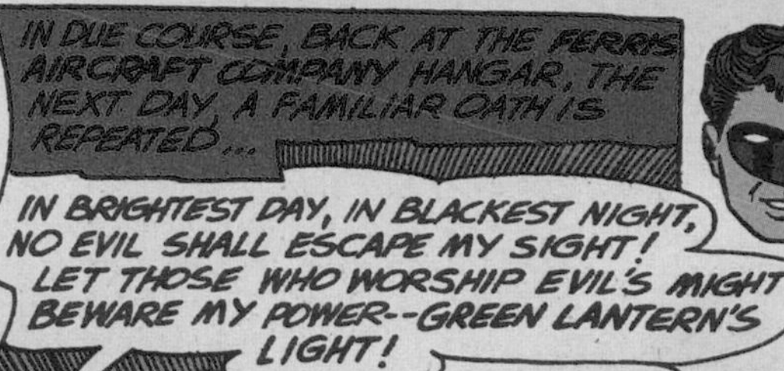

IN DUE COURSE, BACK AT THE FERRIS AIRCRAFT COMPANY HANGAR, THE NEXT DAY, A FAMILIAR OATH IS REPEATED...

IN BRIGHTEST DAY, IN BLACKEST NIGHT, NO EVIL SHALL ESCAPE MY SIGHT! LET THOSE WHO WORSHIP EVIL'S MIGHT BEWARE MY POWER--GREEN LANTERN'S LIGHT!
AH, THAT'S BETTER! IT SURE IS GOOD TO KNOW GREEN LANTERN'S HIM-SELF AGAIN!
The End
THIS IS THE FIRS... OF A PROPOSED SERIE... OF STORIES FEATURING GREE... LANTERN AND THE FLASH WORKING AS A TEAM! IF YOU WOULD LIKE TO SEE MORE OF THIS DYNAMIC DUO IN ACTION, LET US KNOW!